The Impossible Dream

A Yoga Storytelling Adventure

The Impossible Dream

A Yoga Storytelling Adventure

by Kathe Hudson and Melanie Moyer

illustrated by Annabel Jones

Dedications

We would like to dedicate this book to our dad; John Speyrer, whom after growing up in Acadiana made his way to New Orleans to follow his dream and raise his family.
We love you dad. – MM and KH

"Go confidently in the direction of your dreams!"

- Henry David Thoreau

The Impossible Dream is a story that reminds us to have faith in ourselves and to believe in our dreams. This is our version of a folktale that has been told all around the world. Adaptations of this story contain three constants: a dream, a bridge and a treasure.

Born and raised in New Orleans, the authors still reside in the heat and humidity of the swamplands of Louisiana. We are descendants of the Acadians, French Canadians who bravely embarked on their own personal journey to Louisiana in 1765. Our story is set in the heart of Acadiana, and of course the big city where we find the river bridge is New Orleans.

The Impossible Dream depicts the Acadian way of life. Acadians, also known as Cajuns, are hardworking, fun-loving, faithful people who made their homes along the waterways of Louisiana's bayous, rivers and swamplands.

Included is a glossary and Cajun pronunciation guide.

In addition, the book includes options for children to experience a yoga storytelling adventure. We are storytellers and yoga teachers; former librarians, passionate about promoting literacy, health, and wellbeing. We introduce yoga to children through story. Integrating left brain and right brain activity, story and yoga develop language, emotional and physical literacy.

Through the magic of story and the wisdom of yoga it is our sincere hope that children everywhere will remember, **Nothing is Impossible!**

Kathe and Melanie

Cajun Word Fun

Allons (ah LON) = Let's go

Bayou (BYE you) = Slow moving river

Ça fait chaud (sa fay show) = It is hot

Cajun (KAY jun) = A descendent of French Canadians

Couillon (KOO yon) = Crazy, foolish

Fais do do (fay doe doe) = Go to sleep

Je ne connais pas (ja cone A pa) = I don't know

Keeyaw (kee YAW) *draw it out* = Wow

Mon ami (mohn a me) = My friend

Oui (wei) = Yes

Pirogue (PEE rohg) = Small boat

Pooyai (poo YIEE) *draw it out* = Good grief

S'il vous plait (see voo play) = Please

In the song "Goodbye Joe" the word bayou is pronounced BYE-o, it rhymes with Joe, go, and row!

Once upon a time a long time ago or maybe not so long ago… deep down in the swamplands where the air is hot and humid, lived a hardworking young man. He lived in a little cottage with his faithful companions, Max and Joe.

Growing beside the cottage was an old, old oak tree with wispy grey moss hanging from its heavy branches. The oak tree was so old, its gnarly roots pushed up out of the ground lifting up one side of the cottage. But the young man did not mind. He believed life was kind.

Every day he gathered herbs and roots alongside a brown, muddy bayou. With care he placed them in a tattered, red pack. Once it was full he would paddle his pirogue into town to sell his goods. The townspeople called him the Cajun paddler.

One night the paddler had a dream. In the dream a voice softly whispered: "Go to the River Bridge. Go to the River Bridge."

Early the next morning the sun peeked in the window. He sat up in bed, scratched his head and said, "Keeyaw, Wow, what a strange dream. The River Bridge is too far away, I cannot go there—impossible!"

He went about his day completely forgetting about the dream. Happily he hummed a tune, collecting the herbs and roots until the heat of noon. "Ca fait chaud, it sure is hot," the paddler said, while wiping the sweat from his dripping forehead.

Placing the pack in the pirogue, he called out, "Allons, Let's go." Max, ever ready for an adventure, jumped in the pirogue but lazy ole Joe stayed slumped on the porch.

Shoving off, the paddler sang, "Goodbye Joe, me gotta go, me-oh-my-oh. Me gotta go row the pirogue down the bayou."

He sold his goods in town then headed home as the sun dropped below the horizon leaving pink clouds sprinkled like confetti across the sky. The moon came up while he played with his pups. The paddler settled into bed took a deep breath in and out and fell fast asleep.

Once again, he had the very same dream. This time the voice sounded clear as a bell: "Go to the River Bridge. Go to the River Bridge."

Morning arrived. A gentle wind ruffled the window curtain. It tickled his nose and it tickled his toes. He sat up in bed, scratched his head and said, "Keeyaw, Wow, how strange, the same dream two nights in a row. I have too much to do, I cannot go—impossible!"

Straight away he went about his day completely forgetting about the dream. He dug the herbs and roots, wiped his brow then turned to Max with a gracious bow. "Allons, Let's go," and once again Max leaped into the pirogue.

Sly ole Joe, with one eye open, just watched them go.

Shoving off, the paddler sang, "Goodbye Joe, me gotta go, me-oh-my-oh. Me gotta go row the pirogue down the bayou."

He sold his goods in town then paddled home as the sun went down. The moon came up while he played with his pups. The paddler settled into bed, took a deep breath in and out and fell fast asleep.

That night he had the very same dream. "GO TO THE RIVER BRIDGE! GO TO THE RIVER BRIDGE!" The voice was loud as a roar and he fell on the floor.

Scratching his head, the paddler said, "Keeyaw, Wow. Impossible or not, I best give it a shot!"

The paddler provisioned the pirogue. All was set; there was no need to fret.

Shoving off he sang, "Goodbye Joe, me gotta go, me-oh-my-oh. Me gotta go row the pirogue down the bayou."

The sun beamed bright, the day a delight. There was no need to hurry, no reason to worry. He leisurely paddled this way and that way allowing the brown, muddy bayou to lead him to a big, wide river.

Wood doves cooed in the tangled trees. Whistling, the paddler dipped his paddle light as a breeze. "Oui, Yes, this is a mighty fine journey," he thought.

Three days later he reached the bend in the river. What a sight to behold—the River Bridge!

The city was bustling with activity. He had never seen such festivity. Artists were in the square painting portraits. People were coming and going, no one paying him any mind.

Now that he had reached his destination, the paddler did not know what he was supposed to do. Weary from his travels he sat on a worn, weathered bench. He sat and he waited and he sat and he waited and nothing happened.

A scarlet sun slowly sank into the river beneath the River Bridge. As the moon came up the paddler stretched out on the bench. He took a deep breath in and out and spoke tenderly to Max, "Fais dodo mon ami, Go to sleep my friend." Snoring softly, they both slept.

The next day he did the same thing. He sat and he
waited and he sat and he waited and still nothing happened.

Night came. He stretched out on the bench, a blanket of
stars covering him.

When morning broke, the paddler awoke. "Couillon, Crazy! What am I doing?" He picked up his pack, "Max, time to go back."

Just then a merchant all in a stew called out, "Young man s'il vous plait, please wait. I must ask you, why have you been sitting out here day after day? What have you been waiting for?"

The paddler hung his head and with a deep sigh said, "Je ne connais pas, I do not know. I had a dream and in the dream a voice told me to come to the River Bridge. I am here but nothing has happened."

The merchant bent over with a hearty hoot. He laughed so hard tears streamed down his suit. "Pooyai, Good grief, dreams are so silly. Some time ago I too had a dream. I saw a small cottage out in the swamplands and next to it was an old oak tree. The oak tree was so old its roots were pushing up out of the ground lifting up one side of the cottage. In the dream I heard a voice saying, 'Under the oak tree is a treasure.' Imagine me finding a treasure—impossible."

In the blink of an eye, the paddler thanked the merchant and hurried home. He paddled with all his might, he paddled all day, and he paddled all night.

When he got there, he ran to his cottage and began to dig. The old oak tree it was mighty big. He just had to see. What could it be?

What do you think he found under the ground? A treasure of course!

Lifting his hands high to the sky, the paddler realized, NOTHING IS IMPOSSIBLE!

The **Yoga Storytelling** Adventure for Parents and Teachers

Why combine **yoga** and **story**? Story enhances language, listening and critical thinking skills. Yoga enhances body and mind awareness. These twin arts bring balance, strength, and flexibility to body and mind.

Storytelling is extremely valuable in developing young listeners' imaginations and **yoga** brings the **story** alive; it is both interactive and theatrical. By visually acting out the **story** with **yoga** postures, children learn to transfer images into words. Storytelling and **yoga** unite left brain and right brain, both the logical and creative sides are stimulated. Increased engagement promotes deep learning. They are now a part of the **story**, and are able to recall it in detail.

Children are encouraged to use their imaginations, to retell in their own words, enriching and expanding the story's meaning. In other words…to become storytellers!

A **Yoga Storytelling** Adventure for Kids

Let's go on a **yoga storytelling** adventure, we'll use our imaginations and become the paddler, the oak tree, Max the dog, and the pirogue. Acting out the **story** with **yoga** poses will help you to remember the beginning, the middle and the end of the story. You will then be able to retell the story in your own words. Don't forget to paddle your pirogue as your sing, "Goodbye Joe…!"

Practice in your bare feet on a non-slip surface. As with any exercise it is best not to practice immediately after eating. Move slowly into and out of the poses and take slow deep breaths. Above all else have fun!

To end your yoga storytelling adventure, we invite you to sit quietly in Easy Pose with your hands resting on your knees. Close your eyes and breathe in and out slowly and deeply. Take a few quiet moments to consider your dreams. When you are ready open your eyes and remember, "**Nothing is Impossible!**"

Yoga Fun

Mountain pose is the foundational pose from which all other standing poses arise.

Tadasana
Mountain

Stand with feet together, arms by your sides. Press your feet into the ground. Your head, neck and spine are in a straight line reaching high towards the sky.

The Paddler/Warrior II

Virabhadrasana II
Warrior II

Begin in mountain pose. Take a big step back with the left foot. The foot is turned to a 90-degree angle. The shoulders and hips are square to the side. Bend the right knee, with the knee over the ankle. Lift the arms to shoulder height and look out over the right fingertips. Repeat on the other side.

Max/ Downward dog

Adho Mukha Svanasana
Downward Facing Dog

Begin on all fours. Curl the toes as you straighten the legs. Push the hips up. Look at your knees. The back from shoulders to hips should be in a straight line. Return to all fours.

Oak Tree/ Tree pose

Vrksasana
Tree

Begin in mountain pose. Bring the sole of one foot up to the ankle or inner calf, toes pointing to the ground. Balance. Bring the hands together in prayer and slowly reach the arms overhead. Hold the pose as you gaze forward. Repeat on the other side.

Pirogue/ Boat pose

Navasana
Boat

Sit tall, with your legs stretched out in front of you. Bend the knees, holding onto the back of the legs. Now lift the feet off the floor, straightening the legs if possible, and stretch the arms out in front of you.

Paddled this way and that way/ Seated Twist

Marichyasana III
Marichi's Pose III

Sit up tall with legs stretched out in front, with your toes pointing to the sky and your head held high. Bend the right leg. Inhale as you lift the spine and twist to the right, wrapping the left arm around the knee. Exhale as you place the right hand on the floor behind you. Release and return to center and repeat on the other side.

River Bridge/ Bridge pose

Setu Bandhasana
Bridge

Lie on your back, with your knees bent and feet close to the body. Hands are palms-down by the side. Press down on the heels as you slowly lift the hips high. Shoulders press into the ground.

Sat and waited/ Chair pose

Utkatasana
Chair

Stand in mountain pose. Inhale and lift the arms straight overhead and bend the knees.

Bent over laughing/ Forward bend

Uttanasana
Standing Forward Bend

Stand in mountain pose with feet together. Raise arms overhead. Bend forward from the hips, and grasp either the ankles or calves. It's okay to bend the knees! Slowly return to upright.

Ran to cottage/ Lunge

Banarasana
High Lunge

Stand in mountain with feet hip-distance apart. Stretch the left leg back and bend the right knee, with knee over ankle. Reach down and place hands on either side of the knee. The left leg is straight and the toes are curled under. Repeat on the other side.

Nothing is Impossible / Extended Mountain

Utthitta Tadasana
Extended Mountain

Begin in mountain pose. Round the arms overhead, palms facing inward, as you slowly inhale. Look up at your hands as they meet. Turn palms outward and slowly exhale, returning hands to your side.

Sitting Mountain / Easy Pose

Sukhasana
Easy

Sit up tall and cross your legs at the shins, place each foot beneath the opposite knee. Rest your hands on your knees. Align your head, neck and spine. Balance your weight evenly across your sit bones.

Acknowledgements

Jambalaya (On the Bayou) words and music by Hank Williams

copyright© 1952 Sony/ATV Music Publishing LLC
Copyright Renewed
All Rights Administer by Sony/ATV Publishing LLC, 424 Church Street, Suite 1200, Nashville, TN 37219
International Copyright Secured All Rights Reserved
Reprinted by Permission of Hal Leonard LLC

Charlotte Bradley for the beautiful yoga pose illustrations
www.yogaflavoredlife.com

Sydney Solis for the Storytime Yoga® method of storytelling
www.storytimeyoga.com

Erin Couvillion for Cajun word pronunciation guide and editing

Bibliography

The Peddler of Swaffham by Hugh Lipton from "Tales of Wisdom and Wonder," United Kingdom: Barefoot Books, 1998.

The Dream Peddler by Gail E. Haley, New York: Dutton, 1993.

The Peddler's Dream by Sydney Solis, "Storytime Yoga," Boulder: The Mythic Yoga Studio, 2006.

Melanie has a Master's Degree in Library and Information Science. Her experience as a youth services librarian was a catalyst for sharing story and yoga. She is a 200-hour Certified Yoga Teacher as well as a Certified Chair Yoga Teacher. Her passion for sharing yoga extends to all ages.

Kathe has more than 25 years in the fields of Education and Library and Information Science. Story and yoga enchanted her and she became a Master Certified Storytime Yoga Teacher, 200-hour Certified Yoga Teacher, and Certified Chair Yoga Teacher.

Melanie and Kathe are the founders of Moving-Tale, an innovative storytelling and yoga program for children, and are available for school and library presentations. For more information visit us at www.moving-tale.com

Join us on our current yoga storytelling adventures at www.ayogastorytellingadventureblogspot.com

Annabel has a Bachelor's Degree in Art and is working on her Master's in Art at Northwestern State University. She is also a Children's Librarian at a public library! Her main goal in life is to illustrate for children and to one day win a Caldecott (or 2). She lives in Natchitoches, Louisiana with her husband, kids, two cats, and a smelly dog named Izzy.

Made in the USA
San Bernardino, CA
20 November 2017